Miss Snickers' Scavenger Hunt

Dr. Linda Ellington

Interior Image Credit: Valerie Mojica

Archway Publishing books may be ordered through booksellers or by contacting:

Archway Publishing
1663 Liberty Drive
Bloomington, IN 47403
www.archwaypublishing.com
1 (888) 242-5904

ISBN: 978-1-4808-7294-3 (sc)
ISBN: 978-1-4808-7295-0 (hc)
ISBN: 978-1-4808-7293-6 (e)

Print information available on the last page.

Archway Publishing rev. date: 12/21/2018

Miss Snickers' Scavenger Hunt

Grandma says, "OK Miss Snickers, are you
ready to go on a scavenger hunt?"

Yes, barks Miss Snickers, but are
we forgetting something?

Grandma says, "No, we have our net and
our walking shoes on." Here we go!

Grandma says, "Look Miss Snickers, our friend
Mr. Dolphin is swimming in the water by the dock."

Miss Snickers barks hello to Mr. Dolphin.

"Let's look for treasures on our
scavenger hunt," Grandma says.

Miss Snickers looks over the dock into
the water and sees a bottle floating.

"I wonder if there is a pirate's message in the bottle?
Let's put the bottle in our scavenger net,"
Grandma tells Miss Snickers.

Oh, my Miss Snickers, we found another treasure, a tennis ball.

"Where do you think the tennis ball came from?" Grandma asked.

It could be a famous tennis ball that floated over from England. "The Queen plays tennis, you know," Grandma says to Miss Snickers, "who is not sure what an England queen is.

"Oh no, look Miss Snickers, a fishing hook. This could hurt fish if they bite it, as they would not be able to get the hook out of their mouth - what would happen to the fish?"

"Isn't this fun, we picked up treasures on our scavenger hunt, that we can put into the recycle bucket," Grandma says to Miss Snickers.

"We will put the treasures we found into the recycle bucket, so they do not have to stay floating in the water," Grandma says.

"Let's go home Miss Snickers and we will go on another scavenger hunt tomorrow."

Miss Snickers barks and barks as she is happy to be with Grandma walking back home.

Snickers barks and barks as she knows they will adventure on another scavenger hunt, tomorrow.

Dr. Linda Ellington is a college professor and is a member of editorial boards for major textbooks and academic and business journals. She has spent the past two decades studying teaching through storytelling, from pre-school, to college level, and to corporate boardrooms. Ellington lives in Georgia with her best friend, Miss Snickers, a four-legged, little furry creature.

Printed in the United States
By Bookmasters